AN OLD-FASHIONED
THANKSGIVING

LOUISA MAY ALCOTT

AN OLD-FASHIONED
THANKSGIVING

AND OTHER STORIES

penguin books

PENGUIN BOOKS

Published by the Penguin Group

Penguin Books USA Inc., 375 Hudson Street,
New York, New York 10014, U.S.A.
Penguin Books Ltd, 27 Wrights Lane,
London W8 5TZ, England
Penguin Books Australia Ltd, Ringwood,
Victoria, Australia
Penguin Books Canada Ltd, 10 Alcorn Avenue,
Toronto, Ontario, Canada M4V 3B2
Penguin Books (N.Z.) Ltd, 182–190 Wairau Road,
Auckland 10 New Zealand

Penguin Books Ltd, Registered Offices:
Harmondsworth, Middlesex, England

Published in Penguin Books 1995

ISBN 0 14 60.0110 9

Printed in the United States of America

CONTENTS

AN OLD-FASHIONED THANKSGIVING

November, 1881

Sixty years ago, up among the New Hampshire hills, lived Farmer Bassett, with a houseful of sturdy sons and daughters growing up about him. They were poor in money, but rich in land and love, for the wide acres of wood, corn, and pasture land fed, warmed, and clothed the flock, while mutual patience, affection, and courage made the old farmhouse a very happy home.

November had come; the crops were in, and barn, buttery, and bin were overflowing with the harvest that rewarded the summer's hard work. The big kitchen was a jolly place just now, for in the great fireplace roared a cheerful fire; on the walls hung garlands of dried apples, onions, and corn; up aloft from the beams shone crooknecked squashes, juicy hams, and dried venison—for in those days deer still haunted the deep forests, and hunters flourished. Savory smells were in the air; on the crane hung steaming kettles, and down among the red embers copper saucepans simmered, all suggestive of some approaching feast.

A white-headed baby lay in the old blue cradle that had rocked six other babies, now and then lifting his head to 3 look out, like a round, full moon, then subsided to kick and crow contentedly, and suck the rosy apple he had no teeth to bite. Two small boys sat on the wooden settle shelling corn for popping, and picking out the biggest nuts from the goodly store their own hands had gathered in October. Four young girls stood at the long dresser, busily chopping meat, pounding spice, and slicing apples; and the tongues of Tilly, Prue, Roxy, and Rhody went as fast as their hands. Farmer Bassett, and Eph, the oldest boy, were "chorin' 'round" outside, for Thanksgiving was at hand, and all must be in order for that time-honored day.

To and fro, from table to hearth, bustled buxom Mrs. Bassett, flushed and floury, but busy and blithe as the queen bee of this busy little hive should be.

"I do like to begin seasonable and have things to my mind. Thanksgivin' dinners can't be drove, and it does take a sight of victuals to fill all these hungry stomicks," said the good woman, as she gave a vigorous stir to the great kettle of cider applesauce, and cast a glance of housewifely pride at the fine array of pies set forth on the buttery shelves.

"Only one more day and then it will be the time to eat. I didn't take but one bowl of hasty pudding this morning, so I shall have plenty of room when the nice things come," confided Seth to Sol, as he cracked a large hazelnut as easily as a squirrel.

"No need of my starvin' beforehand. *I always* have room enough, and I'd like to have Thanksgiving every day," answered Solomon, gloating like a young ogre over the little pig that lay near by, ready for roasting.

"Sakes alive, I don't, boys! It's a marcy it don't come but once a year. I should be worn to a thread paper with all this extra work atop of my winter weavin' and spinnin'," laughed their mother, as she plunged her plump arms into the long bread trough and began to knead the dough as if a famine were at hand.

Tilly, the oldest girl, a red-cheeked, black-eyed lass of fourteen, was grinding briskly at the mortar, for spices were costly, and not a grain must be wasted. Prue kept time with the chopper, and the twins sliced away at the apples till their little brown arms ached, for all knew how to work, and did so now with a will.

"I think it's real fun to have Thanksgiving at home. I'm sorry Gran'ma is sick, so we can't go there as usual, but I like to mess 'round here, don't you, girls?" asked Tilly, pausing to take a sniff at the spicy pestle.

"It will be kind of lonesome with only our own folks." "I like to see all the cousins and aunts, and have games, and sing," cried the twins, who were regular little romps, and could run, swim, coast, and shout as well as their brothers.

"I don't care a mite for all that. It will be so nice to eat 5 dinner together, warm and comfortable at home," said quiet Prue, who loved her own cozy nooks like a cat.

"Come, girls, fly 'round and get your chores done, so we can clear away for dinner jest as soon as I clap my bread into the oven," called Mrs. Bassett presently, as she rounded off the last loaf of brown bread which was to feed the hungry mouths that seldom tasted any other.

"Here's a man comin' up the hill lively!" "Guess it's Gad Hopkins. Pa told him to bring a dezzen oranges, if they warn't too high!" shouted Sol and Seth, running to the door, while the girls smacked their lips at the thought of this rare treat, and Baby threw his apple overboard, as if getting ready for a new cargo.

But all were doomed to disappointment, for it was not Gad, with the much-desired fruit. It was a stranger, who threw himself off his horse and hurried up to Mr. Bassett in the yard, with some brief message that made the farmer drop his ax and look so sober that his wife guessed at once some bad news had come; and crying, "Mother's wuss! I know she is!" Out ran the good woman, forgetful of the flour on her arms and the oven waiting for its most important batch.

The man said old Mr. Chadwick, down to Keene, stopped him as he passed, and told him to tell Mrs. Bassett her mother was failin' fast, and she'd better come today. He knew no more, and having delivered his errand he rode away, saying it looked like snow and he must be jogging, or he wouldn't get home till night.

"We must go right off, Eldad. Hitch up, and I'll be ready in less'n no time," said Mrs. Bassett, wasting not a minute in tears and lamentations, but pulling off her apron as she went in, with her head in a sad jumble of bread, anxiety, turkey, sorrow, haste, and cider applesauce.

A few words told the story, and the children left their work to help her get ready, mingling their grief for "Gran'ma" with regrets for the lost dinner.

"I'm dreadful sorry, dears, but it can't be helped. I couldn't cook nor eat no way now, and if that blessed woman gets better sudden, as she has before, we'll have cause for thanksgivin', and I'll give you a dinner you won't forget in a hurry," said Mrs. Bassett, as she tied on her brown silk pumpkin-hood, with a sob for the good old mother who had made it for her.

Not a child complained after that, but ran about helpfully, bringing moccasins, heating the footstone, and getting ready for a long drive, because Gran'ma lived twenty miles away, and there were no railroads in those parts to whisk people to and fro like magic. By the time the old yellow sleigh was at the door, the bread was in the oven, and Mrs. Bassett was waiting, with her camlet cloak on, and the baby done up like a small bale of blankets.

"Now, Eph, you must look after the cattle like a man, and keep up the fires, for there's a storm brewin', and 7 neither the children nor dumb critters must suffer," said Mr. Bassett, as he turned up the collar of his rough coat and put on his blue mittens, while the old mare shook her bells as if she preferred a trip to Keene to hauling wood all day.

"Tilly, put extry comfortables on the beds to-night, the wind is so searchin' up chamber. Have the baked beans and Injun-puddin' for dinner, and whatever you do, don't let the boys get at the mince-pies, or you'll have them down sick. I shall come back the minute I can leave Mother. Pa will come to-morrer anyway, so keep snug and be good. I depend on you, my darter; use your jedgment, and don't let nothin' happen while Mother's away."

"Yes'm, yes'm—good-bye, good-bye!" called the children, as Mrs. Bassett was packed into the sleigh and driven away, leaving a stream of directions behind her.

Eph, the sixteen-year-old boy, immediately put on his biggest boots, assumed a sober, responsible manner, and surveyed his little responsibilities with a paternal air, drolly like his father's. Tilly tied on her mother's bunch of keys, rolled up the sleeves of her homespun gown, and began to order about the younger girls. They soon forgot poor Granny, and found it great fun to keep house all alone, for Mother seldom left home, but ruled her family in the good old-fashioned way. There were no servants, for the little daughters were Mrs. Bassett's only maids, and the stout boys helped their father, all working happily together with no wages but love; learning in the best manner the use of the heads and hands with which they were to make their own way in the world.

The few flakes that caused the farmer to predict bad weather soon increased to a regular snowstorm, with gusts of wind, for up among the hills winter came early and lingered long. But the children were busy, gay, and warm indoors, and never minded the rising gale nor the whirling white storm outside.

Tilly got them a good dinner, and when it was over the two elder girls went to their spinning, for in the kitchen stood the big and little wheels, and baskets of wool rolls ready to be twisted into yarn for the winter's knitting, and each day brought its stint of work to the daughters, who hoped to be as thrifty as their mother.

Eph kept up a glorious fire, and superintended the small boys, who popped corn and whittled boats on the hearth; while Roxy and Rhody dressed corncob dolls in the settle corner, and Bose, the brindled mastiff, lay on the braided mat, luxuriously warming his old legs. Thus employed, they made a pretty picture, these rosy boys and girls, in their homespun suits, with the rustic toys or tasks which most children nowadays would find very poor or tiresome.

Tilly and Prue sang, as they stepped to and fro, drawing out the smoothly twisted threads to the musical hum of the great spinning wheels. The little girls chattered like magpies over their dolls and the new bedspread they were planning to make, all white dimity stars on a blue calico ground, as a Christmas present to Ma. The boys roared at Eph's jokes, and had rough and tumble games over Bose, who didn't mind them in the least; and so the afternoon wore pleasantly away.

At sunset the boys went out to feed the cattle, bring in heaps of wood, and lock up for the night, as the lonely farmhouse seldom had visitors after dark. The girls got the simple supper of brown bread and milk, baked apples, and a doughnut all 'round as a treat. Then they sat before the fire, the sisters knitting, the brothers with books or games, for Eph loved reading, and Sol and Seth never failed to play a few games of Morris with barley corns, on the little board they had themselves at one corner of the dresser.

"Read out a piece," said Tilly from Mother's chair, where she sat in state, finishing off the sixth woolen sock she had knit that month.

"It's the old history book, but here's a bit you may like, since it's about our folks," answered Eph, turning the yellow page to look at a picture of two quaintly dressed children in some ancient castle.

"Yes, read that. I always like to hear about the Lady Matildy I was named for, and Lord Bassett, Pa's great-great-great grandpa. He's only a farmer now, but it's nice to know we were somebody two or three hundred years ago," said Tilly, bridling and tossing her curly head as she fancied the Lady Matilda might have done.

"Don't read the queer words, 'cause we don't understand 'em. Tell it," commanded Roxy, from the cradle, where she was drowsily cuddled with Rhody.

"Well, a long time ago, when Charles the First was in prison, Lord Bassett was a true friend to him," began Eph, plunging into his story without delay. "The lord had some papers that would have hung a lot of people if the king's enemies got hold of 'em, so when he heard one day, all of a sudden, that soldiers were at the castle gate to carry him off, he had just time to call his girl to him and say: 'I may be going to my death, but I won't betray my master. There is no time to burn the papers, and I can not take them with me; they are hidden in the old leathern chair where I sit. No one knows this but you, and you must guard them till I come or send you a safe messenger to take them away. Promise me to be brave and silent, and I can go without fear.' You see, he wasn't afraid to die, but he *was* to seem a traitor. Lady Matildy promised solemnly, and the words were hardly out of her mouth when the men came in, and her father was carried away a prisoner and sent off to the Tower."

"But she didn't cry; she just called her brother, and sat down in that chair, with her head leaning back on those papers, like a queen, and waited while the soldiers hunted the house over for 'em: wasn't that a smart girl?" cried 11

Tilly, beaming with pride, for she was named for this ancestress, and knew the story by heart.

"I reckon she was scared, though, when the men came swearin' in and asked her if she knew anything about it. The boy did his part then, for *he* didn't know, and fired up and stood before his sister; and he says, says he, as bold as a lion: 'If my lord had told us where the papers be, we would die before we would betray him. But we are children and know nothing, and it is cowardly of you to try to fight us with oaths and drawn swords!'"

As Eph quoted from the book, Seth planted himself before Tilly, with the long poker in his hand, saying, as he flourished it valiantly:

"Why didn't the boy take his father's sword and lay about him? I would, if any one was ha'sh to Tilly."

"You bantam! He was only a bit of a boy, and couldn't do anything. Sit down and hear the rest of it," commanded Tilly, with a pat on the yellow head, and a private resolve that Seth should have the largest piece of pie at dinner next day, as reward for his chivalry.

"Well, the men went off after turning the castle out of window, but they said they should come again; so faithful Matildy was full of trouble, and hardly dared to leave the room where the chair stood. All day she sat there, and at night her sleep was so full of fear about it, that she often got up and went to see that all was safe. The servants thought the fright had hurt her wits, and let her be, but

Rupert, the boy, stood by her and never was afraid of her queer ways. She was 'a pious maid,' the book says, and often spent the long evenings reading the Bible, with her brother by her, all alone in the great room, with no one to help her bear her secret, and no good news of her father. At last, word came that the king was dead and his friends banished out of England. Then the poor children were in a sad plight, for they had no mother, and the servants all ran away, leaving only one faithful old man to help them."

"But the father did come?" cried Roxy, eagerly.

"You'll see," continued Eph, half telling, half reading.

"Matilda was sure he would, so she sat on in the big chair, guarding the papers, and no one could get her away, till one day a man came with her father's ring and told her to give up the secret. She knew the ring, but would not tell until she had asked many questions, so as to be very sure, and while the man answered all about her father and the king, she looked at him sharply. Then she stood up and said, in a tremble, for there was something strange about the man: 'Sir, I doubt you in spite of the ring, and I will not answer till you pull off the false beard you wear, that I may see your face and know if you are my father's friend or foe.' Off came the disguise, and Matilda found it was my lord himself, come to take them with him out of England. He was very proud of that faithful girl, I guess, for the old chair still stands in the castle, and the 13 name keeps in the family, Pa says, even over here, where some of the Bassetts came along with the Pilgrims."

"Our Tilly would have been as brave, I know, and she looks like the old picter down to Gran'ma's, don't she, Eph?" cried Prue, who admired her bold, bright sister very much.

"Well, I think you'd do the settin' part best, Prue, you are so patient. Till would fight like a wild cat, but she can't hold her tongue worth a cent," answered Eph; whereat Tilly pulled his hair, and the story ended with a general frolic.

When the moon-faced clock behind the door struck nine, Tilly tucked up the children under the "extry comfortables," and having kissed them all around, as Mother did, crept into her own nest, never minding the little drifts of snow that sifted in upon her coverlet between the shingles of the roof, nor the storm that raged without.

As if he felt the need of unusual vigilance, old Bose lay down on the mat before the door, and pussy had the warm hearth all to herself. If any late wanderer had looked in at midnight, he would have seen the fire blazing up again, and in the cheerful glow the old cat blinking her yellow eyes, as she sat bolt upright beside the spinning wheel, like some sort of household goblin, guarding the children while they slept.

When they woke, like early birds, it still snowed, but
up the little Bassetts jumped, broke the ice in their jugs,

and went down with cheeks glowing like winter apples, after a brisk scrub and scramble into their clothes. Eph was off to the barn, and Tilly soon had a great kettle of mush ready, which, with milk warm from the cows made a wholesome breakfast for the seven hearty children.

"Now about dinner," said the young housekeeper, as the pewter spoons stopped clattering, and the earthen bowls stood empty.

"Ma said, have what we liked, but she didn't expect us to have a real Thanksgiving dinner, because she won't be here to cook it, and we don't know how," began Prue, doubtfully.

"I can roast a turkey and make a pudding as well as anybody, I guess. The pies are all ready, and if we can't boil vegetables and so on, we don't deserve any dinner," cried Tilly, burning to distinguish herself, and bound to enjoy to the utmost her brief authority.

"Yes, yes!" cried all the boys, "let's have a dinner anyway; Ma won't care, and the good victuals will spoil if they ain't eaten right up."

"Pa is coming tonight, so we won't have dinner till late; that will be real genteel and give us plenty of time," added Tilly, suddenly realizing the novelty of the task she had undertaken.

"Did you ever roast a turkey?" asked Roxy, with an air of deep interest.

"Should you darst to try?" said Rhody, in an awe-stricken tone.

"You will see what I can do. Ma said I was to use my judgment about things, and I'm going to. All you children have got to do is to keep out of the way, and let Prue and me work. Eph, I wish you'd put a fire in the best room, so the little ones can play in there. We shall want the settin'-room for the table, and I won't have them pickin' 'round when we get things fixed," commanded Tilly, bound to make her short reign a brilliant one.

"I don't know about that. Ma didn't tell us to," began cautious Eph who felt that this invasion of the sacred best parlor was a daring step.

"Don't we always do it Sundays and Thanksgivings? Wouldn't Ma wish the children kept safe and warm anyhow? Can I get up a nice dinner with four rascals under my feet all the time? Come, now, if you want roast turkey and onions, plum-puddin' and mince-pie, you'll have to do as I tell you, and be lively about it."

Tilly spoke with such spirit, and her suggestion was so irresistible, that Eph gave in, and, laughing good-naturedly, tramped away to heat up the best room, devoutly hoping that nothing serious would happen to punish such audacity.

The young folks delightedly trooped away to destroy the order of that prim apartment with housekeeping under the black horsehair sofa, "horseback-riders" on the arms of the best rocking chair, and an Indian war dance all over the well-waxed furniture. Eph, finding the society of peaceful sheep and cows more to his mind than that of two excited sisters, lingered over his chores in the barn as long as possible, and left the girls in peace.

Now Tilly and Prue were in their glory, and as soon as the breakfast things were out of the way, they prepared for a grand cooking time. They were handy girls, though they had never heard of a cooking school, never touched a piano, and knew nothing of embroidery beyond the samplers which hung framed in the parlor; one ornamented with a pink mourner under a blue weeping willow, the other with this pleasing verse, each word being done in a different color, which gave the effect of a distracted rainbow:

> This sampler neat was worked by me,
> In my twelfth year, Prudence B.

Both rolled up their sleeves, put on their largest aprons, and got out all the spoons, dishes, pots, and pans they could find, "so as to have everything handy," Prue said.

"Now, sister, we'll have dinner at five; Pa will be here by that time, if he is coming tonight, and be so surprised to find us all ready, for he won't have had any very nice victuals if Gran'ma is so sick," said Tilly, importantly. "I shall give the children a piece at noon" (Tilly meant 17 luncheon); "doughnuts and cheese, with apple pie and cider, will please 'em. There's beans for Eph; he likes cold pork, so we won't stop to warm it up, for there's lots to do, and I don't mind saying to you I'm dreadful dubersome about the turkey."

"It's all ready but the stuffing, and roasting is as easy as can be. I can baste first-rate. Ma always likes to have me, I'm so patient and stiddy, she says," answered Prue, for the responsibility of this great undertaking did not rest upon her, so she took a cheerful view of things.

"I know, but it's the stuffin' that troubles me," said Tilly, rubbing her round elbows as she eyed the immense fowl laid out on a platter before her. "I don't know how much I want, nor what sort of yarbs to put in, and he's so awful big, I'm kind of afraid of him."

"I ain't! I fed him all summer, and he never gobbled at *me*. I feel real mean to be thinking of gobbling him, poor old chap," laughed Prue, patting her departed pet with an air of mingled affection and appetite.

"Well, I'll get the puddin' off my mind fust, for it ought to bile all day. Put the big kettle on, and see that the spit is clean, while I get ready."

Prue obediently tugged away at the crane, with its black hooks, from which hung the iron teakettle and three-legged pot; then she settled the long spit in the grooves made for it in the tall andirons, and put the dripping pan underneath, for in those days meat was roasted as it should be, not baked in ovens.

Meantime Tilly attacked the plum pudding. She felt pretty sure of coming out right, here, for she had seen her mother do it so many times, it looked very easy. So in went suet and fruit; all sorts of spice, to be sure she got the right ones, and brandy instead of wine. But she forgot both sugar and salt, and tied it in the cloth so tightly that it had no room to swell, so it would come out as heavy as lead and as hard as a cannonball, if the bag did not burst and spoil it all. Happily unconscious of these mistakes, Tilly popped it into the pot, and proudly watched it bobbing about before she put the cover on and left it to its fate.

"I can't remember what flavorin' Ma puts in," she said, when she had got her bread well soaked for stuffing. "Sage and onions and applesauce go with goose, but I can't feel sure of anything but pepper and salt for a turkey."

"Ma puts in some kind of mint, I know, but I forget whether it is spearmint, peppermint, or pennyroyal," answered Prue, in a tone of doubt, but trying to show her knowledge of "yarbs," or, at least, of their names.

"Seems to me it's sweet majoram or summer savory. I guess we'll put both in, and then we are sure to be right. The best is up garret; you run and get some, while I mash the bread," commanded Tilly, diving into the mess.

Away trotted Prue, but in her haste she got catnip and wormwood, for the garret was darkish, and Prue's little nose was so full of the smell of the onions she had been peeling, that everything smelt of them. Eager to be of use, she pounded up the herbs and scattered the mixture with a liberal hand into the bowl.

"It doesn't smell just right, but I suppose it will when it is cooked," said Tilly, as she filled the empty stomach, that seemed aching for food, and sewed it up with the blue yarn, which happened to be handy. She forgot to tie down his legs and wings, but she set him by till his hour came, well satisfied with her work.

"Shall we roast the little pig, too? I think he'd look nice with a necklace of sausages, as Ma fixed him at Christmas," asked Prue, elated with their success.

"I couldn't do it. I loved that little pig, and cried when he was killed. I should feel as if I was roasting the baby," answered Tilly, glancing toward the buttery where piggy hung, looking so pink and pretty it certainly did seem cruel to eat him.

It took a long time to get all the vegetables ready, for, as the cellar was full, the girls thought they would have every sort. Eph helped, and by noon all was ready for cooking, and the cranberry sauce, a good deal scorched, was cooking in the lean-to.

Luncheon was a lively meal, and doughnuts and cheese 20 vanished in such quantities that Tilly feared no one would have an appetite for her sumptuous dinner. The boys assured her they would be starving by five o'clock, and Sol mourned bitterly over the little pig that was not to be served up.

"Now you all go and coast, while Prue and I set the table and get out the best chiny," said Tilly, bent on having her dinner look well, no matter what its other failings might be.

Out came the rough sleds, on went the round hoods, old hats, red cloaks, and moccasins, and away trudged the four younger Bassetts, to disport themselves in the snow, and try the ice down by the old mill, where the great wheel turned and splashed so merrily in the summertime.

Eph took his fiddle and scraped away to his heart's content in the parlor, while the girls, after a short rest, set the table and made all ready to dish up the dinner when that exciting moment came. It was not at all the sort of table we see now, but would look very plain and countrified to us, with its green-handled knives, and two-pronged steel forks, its red-and-white china, and pewter platters, scoured till they shone, with mugs and spoons to match, and a brown jug for the cider. The cloth was coarse, but white as snow, and the little maids had seen the blue-eyed flax grow, out of which their mother wove the linen; they had watched and watched while it bleached in the green meadow. They had no napkins and little silver; but the best tankard and Ma's few wedding spoons were set forth in state. Nuts and apples at the corners gave an air, and the place of honor was left in the middle for the oranges yet to come.

"Don't it look beautiful?" said Prue, when they paused to admire the general effect.

"Pretty nice, I think. I wish Ma could see how well we can do it," began Tilly, when a loud howling startled both girls, and sent them flying to the window. The short afternoon had passed so quickly that twilight had come before they knew it, and now, as they looked out through the gathering dusk, they saw four small black figures tearing up the road, to come bursting in, all screaming at once: "The bear, the bear! Eph, get the gun! He's coming, he's coming!"

Eph had dropped his fiddle, and got down his gun before the girls could calm the children enough to tell their story, which they did in a somewhat incoherent manner. "Down in the holler, coastin', we heard a growl," began Sol, with his eyes as big as saucers. "I see him fust lookin' over the wall," roared Seth, eager to get his share of honor.

"Awful big and shaggy," quavered Roxy, clinging to Tilly, while Rhody hid in Prue's skirts, and piped out: "His great paws kept clawing at us, and I was so scared my legs would hardly go."

"We ran away as fast as we could go, and he came growlin' after us. He's awful hungry, and he'll eat every one of us if he gets in," continued Sol, looking about him for a safe retreat.

"Oh, Eph, don't let him eat us," cried both little girls, flying upstairs to hide under their mother's bed, as their surest shelter.

"No danger of that, you little geese. I'll shoot him as soon as he comes. Get out of the way, boys," and Eph raised the window to get good aim.

"There he is! Fire away, and don't miss!" cried Seth, hastily following Sol, who had climbed to the top of the dresser as a good perch from which to view the approaching fray.

Prue retired to the hearth as if bent on dying at her post rather than desert the turkey, now "browning beautiful," as she expressed it. But Tilly boldly stood at the open window, ready to lend a hand if the enemy proved too much for Eph.

All had seen bears, but none had ever come so near before, and even brave Eph felt that the big brown beast slowly trotting up the dooryard was an unusually formidable specimen. He was growling horribly, and stopped now and then as if to rest and shake himself.

"Get the ax, Tilly, and if I should miss, stand ready to keep him off while I load again," said Eph, anxious to kill his first bear in style and alone; a girl's help didn't count.

Tilly flew for the ax, and was at her brother's side by the time the bear was near enough to be dangerous. He 23 stood on his hind legs, and seemed to sniff with relish the savory odors that poured out of the window.

"Fire, Eph!" cried Tilly, firmly.

"Wait till he rears again. I'll get a better shot then," answered the boy, while Prue covered her ears to shut out the bang, and the small boys cheered from their dusty refuge among the pumpkins.

But a very singular thing happened next, and all who saw it stood amazed, for suddenly Tilly threw down the ax, flung open the door, and ran straight into the arms of the bear, who stood erect to receive her, while his growlings changed to a loud "Haw, haw!" that startled the children more than the report of a gun.

"It's Gad Hopkins, tryin' to fool us!" cried Eph, much disgusted at the loss of his prey, for these hardy boys loved to hunt and prided themselves on the number of wild animals and birds they could shoot in a year.

"Oh, Gad, how could you scare us so?" laughed Tilly, still held fast in one shaggy arm of the bear, while the other drew a dozen oranges from some deep pocket in the buffalo-skin coat, and fired them into the kitchen with such good aim that Eph ducked, Prue screamed, and Sol and Seth came down much quicker than they went up.

"Wal, you see I got upsot over yonder, and the old horse went home while I was floundering in a drift, so I tied on the buffalers to tote 'em easy, and come along till I see the children playin' in the holler. I jest meant to give

'em a little scare, but they run like partridges, and I kep'
up the joke to see how Eph would like this sort of company," and Gad haw-hawed again.

"You'd have had a warm welcome if we hadn't found
you out. I'd have put a bullet through you in a jiffy, old
chap," said Eph, coming out to shake hands with the
young giant, who was only a year or two older than himself.

"Come in and set up to dinner with us. Prue and I have
done it all ourselves, and Pa will be along soon, I reckon,"
cried Tilly, trying to escape.

"Couldn't, no ways. My folks will think I'm dead ef I
don't get along home, sence the horse and sleigh have
gone ahead empty. I've done my arrant and had my joke;
now I want my pay, Tilly," and Gad took a hearty kiss
from the rosy cheeks of his "little sweetheart," as he
called her. His own cheeks tingled with the smart slap she
gave him as she ran away, calling out that she hated bears
and would bring her ax next time.

"I ain't afeared—your sharp eyes found me out: and ef
you run into a bear's arms you must expect a hug," answered Gad, as he pushed back the robe and settled his
fur cap more becomingly.

"I should have known you in a minute if I hadn't been
asleep when the girls squalled. You did it well, though,
and I advise you not to try it again in a hurry, or you'll 25

get shot," said Eph, as they parted, he rather crestfallen and Gad in high glee.

"My sakes alive—the turkey is all burnt one side, and the kettles have biled over so the pies I put to warm are all ashes!" scolded Tilly, as the flurry subsided and she remembered her dinner.

"Well, I can't help it. I couldn't think of victuals when I expected to be eaten alive myself, could I?" pleaded poor Prue, who had tumbled into the cradle when the rain of oranges began.

Tilly laughed, and all the rest joined in, so goodhumor was restored, and the spirits of the younger ones were revived by sucks from the one orange which passed from hand to hand with great rapidity while the older girls dished up the dinner. They were just struggling to get the pudding out of the cloth when Roxy called out: "Here's Pa!"

"There's folks with him," added Rhody.

"Lots of 'em! I see two big sleighs chock full," shouted Seth, peering through the dusk.

"It looks like a seminary. Guess Gran'ma's dead and come up to be buried here," said Sol, in a solemn tone. This startling suggestion made Tilly, Prue, and Eph hasten to look out, full of dismay at such an ending of their festival.

26   "If that is a funeral, the mourners are uncommonly

jolly," said Eph, dryly, as merry voices and loud laughter broke the white silence without.

"I see Aunt Cinthy, and Cousin Hetty—and there's Mose and Amos. I do declare, Pa's bringin' 'em all home to have some fun here," cried Prue, as she recognized one familiar face after another.

"Oh, my patience! Ain't I glad I got dinner, and don't I hope it will turn out good!" exclaimed Tilly, while the twins pranced with delight, and the small boys roared:

"Hooray for Pa! Hooray for Thanksgivin'!"

The cheer was answered heartily, and in came Father, Mother, Baby, aunts, and cousins, all in great spirits, and all much surprised to find such a festive welcome awaiting them.

"Ain't Gran'ma dead at all?" asked Sol, in the midst of the kissing and handshaking.

"Bless your heart, no! It was all a mistake of old Mr. Chadwick's. He's as deaf as an adder, and when Mrs. Brooks told him Mother was mendin' fast, and she wanted me to come down today, certain sure, he got the message all wrong, and give it to the fust person passin' in such a way as to scare me 'most to death, and send us down in a hurry. Mother was sittin' up as chirk as you please, and dreadful sorry you didn't all come."

"So, to keep the house quiet for her, and give you a taste of the fun, your Pa fetched us all up to spend the evenin', and we are goin' to have a jolly time on't, to jedge 27 by the looks of things," said Aunt Cinthy, briskly finishing the tale when Mrs. Bassett paused for want of breath.

"What in the world put it into your head we was comin', and set you to gittin' up such a supper?" asked Mr. Bassett, looking about him, well pleased and much surprised at the plentiful table.

Tilly modestly began to tell, but the others broke in and sang her praises in a sort of chorus, in which bears, pigs, pies, and oranges were oddly mixed. Great satisfaction was expressed by all, and Tilly and Prue were so elated by the commendation of Ma and the aunts, that they set forth their dinner, sure everything was perfect.

But when the eating began, which it did the moment wraps were off, then their pride got a fall; for the first person who tasted the stuffing (it was big Cousin Mose, and that made it harder to bear) nearly choked over the bitter morsel.

"Tilly Bassett, whatever made you put wormwood and catnip in your stuffin'?" demanded Ma, trying not to be severe, for all the rest were laughing, and Tilly looked ready to cry.

"I did it," said Prue, nobly taking all the blame, which caused Pa to kiss her on the spot, and declare that it didn't do a mite of harm, for the turkey was all right.

"I never see onions cooked better. All the vegetables is 28 well done, and the dinner a credit to you, my dears," declared Aunt Cinthy, with her mouth full of the fragrant vegetable she praised.

The pudding was an utter failure in spite of the blazing brandy in which it lay—as hard and heavy as one of the stone balls on Squire Dunkin's great gate. It was speedily whisked out of sight, and all fell upon the pies, which were perfect. But Tilly and Prue were much depressed, and didn't recover their spirits till dinner was over and the evening fun well under way.

"Blind-man's bluff," "Hunt the slipper," "Come, Philander," and other lively games soon set everyone bubbling over with jollity, and when Eph struck up "Money Musk" on his fiddle, old and young fell into their places for a dance. All down the long kitchen they stood, Mr. and Mrs. Bassett at the top, the twins at the bottom, and then away they went, heeling and toeing, cutting pigeon-wings, and taking their steps in a way that would convulse modern children with their new-fangled romps called dancing. Mose and Tilly covered themselves with glory by the vigor with which they kept it up, till fat Aunt Cinthy fell into a chair, breathlessly declaring that a very little of such exercise was enough for a woman of her "heft."

Apples and cider, chat and singing, finished the evening, and after a grand kissing all round, the guests drove away in the clear moonlight which came out to cheer their long drive.

When the jingle of the last bell had died away, Mr.

Bassett said soberly, as they stood together on the hearth: "Children, we have special cause to be thankful that the sorrow we expected was changed into joy, so we'll read a chapter 'fore we go to bed, and give thanks where thanks is due."

Then Tilly set out the light stand with the big Bible on it, and a candle on each side, and all sat quietly in the firelight, smiling as they listened with happy hearts to the sweet old words that fit all times and seasons so beautifully.

When the good-nights were over, and the children in bed, Prue put her arm round Tilly and whispered tenderly, for she felt her shake, and was sure she was crying:

"Don't mind about the old stuffin' and puddin', deary—nobody cared, and Ma said we really did do surprisin' well for such young girls."

The laughter Tilly was trying to smother broke out then, and was so infectious, Prue could not help joining her, even before she knew the cause of the merriment.

"I was mad about the mistakes, but don't care enough to cry. I'm laughing to think how Gad fooled Eph and I found him out. I thought Mose and Amos would have died over it, when I told them, it was so funny," explained Tilly, when she got her breath.

"I was so scared that when the first orange hit me, I 30 thought it was a bullet, and scrabbled into the cradle as fast as I could. It was real mean to frighten the little ones so," laughed Prue, as Tilly gave a growl.

Here a smart rap on the wall of the next room caused a sudden lull in the fun, and Mrs. Bassett's voice was heard, saying warningly, "Girls, go to sleep immediate, or you'll wake the baby."

"Yes'm," answered two meek voices, and after a few irrepressible giggles, silence reigned, broken only by an occasional snore from the boys, or the soft scurry of mice in the buttery, taking their part in this old-fashioned Thanksgiving.

How I Went Out
to Service

When I was eighteen I wanted something to do. I had tried teaching for two years, and hated it; I had tried sewing, and could not earn my bread in that way, at the cost of health; I tried story-writing and got five dollars for stories which now bring a hundred; I had thought seriously of going upon the stage, but certain highly respectable relatives were so shocked at the mere idea that I relinquished my dramatic aspirations.

"What *shall* I do?" was still the question that perplexed me. I was ready to work, eager to be independent, and too proud to endure patronage. But the right task seemed hard to find, and my bottled energies were fermenting in a way that threatened an explosion before long.

My honored mother was a city missionary that winter, and not only served the clamorous poor, but often found it in her power to help decayed gentlefolk by quietly placing them where they could earn their bread without the entire sacrifice of taste and talent which makes poverty so hard for such to bear. Knowing her tact and skill, people often came to her for companions, housekeepers, and that 35 class of the needy who do not make their wants known through an intelligence office.

One day, as I sat dreaming splendid dreams, while I made a series of little petticoats out of the odds and ends sent in for the poor, a tall, ministerial gentleman appeared, in search of a companion for his sister. He possessed an impressive nose, a fine flow of language, and a pair of large hands, encased in black kid gloves. With much waving of these somber members, Mr. R. set forth the delights awaiting the happy soul who should secure this home. He described it as a sort of heaven on earth. "There are books, pictures, flowers, a piano, and the best of society," he said. "This person will be one of the family in all respects, and only required to help about the lighter work, which my sister has done herself hitherto, but is now a martyr to neuralgia and needs a gentle friend to assist her."

My mother, who never lost her faith in human nature, in spite of many impostures, believed every word, and quite beamed with benevolent interest as she listened and tried to recall some needy young woman to whom this charming home would be a blessing. I also innocently thought:

"That sounds inviting. I like housework and can do it well. I should have time to enjoy the books and things I love, and D——is not far away from home. Suppose I try it."

So, when my mother turned to me, asking if I could suggest any one, I became as red as a poppy and said abruptly:

"Only myself."

"Do you really mean it?" cried my astonished parent.

"I really do if Mr. R. thinks I should suit" was my steady reply, as I partially obscured my crimson countenance behind a little flannel skirt, still redder.

The Reverend Josephus gazed upon me with the benign regard which a bachelor of five and thirty may accord a bashful damsel of eighteen. A smile dawned upon his countenance, "sicklied o'er with the pale cast of thought," or dyspepsia; and he softly folded the black gloves, as if about to bestow a blessing as he replied, with emphasis:

"I am sure you would, and we should think ourselves most fortunate if we could secure your society, and—ahem—services for my poor sister."

"Then I'll try it," responded the impetuous maid.

"We will talk it over a little first, and let you know tomorrow, sir," put in my prudent parent, adding, as Mr. R. arose: "What wages do you pay?"

"My dear madam, in a case like this let me not use such words as those. Anything you may think proper we shall gladly give. The labor is very light, for there are but three of us and our habits are of the simplest sort. I am a frail reed and may break at any moment; so is my sister, and my aged father cannot long remain; therefore, money is little to us, and any one who comes to lend her youth and strength to our feeble household will not be forgotten in the end, I assure you." And, with another pensive smile, a farewell wave of the impressive gloves, the Reverend Josephus bowed like a well-sweep and departed.

"My dear, are you in earnest?" asked my mother.

"Of course, I am. Why not try this experiment? It can but fail, like all the others."

"I have no objection; only I fancied you were rather too proud for this sort of thing."

"I am too proud to be idle and dependent, ma'am. I'll scrub floors and take in washing first. I do housework at home for love; why not do it abroad for money? I like it better than teaching. It is healthier than sewing and surer than writing. So why not try it?"

"It is going out to service, you know, though you are called a companion. How does that suit?"

"I don't care. Every sort of work that is paid for is service; and I don't mind being a companion, if I can do it well. I may find it is my mission to take care of neuralgic old ladies and lackadaisical clergymen. It does not sound exciting, but it's better than nothing," I answered, with a sigh; for it *was* rather a sudden downfall to give up being a Siddons and become a Betcinder.

How my sisters laughed when they heard the new plan! But they soon resigned themselves, sure of fun, for Lu's adventures were the standing joke of the family. Of course, the highly respectable relatives held up their hands in holy horror at the idea of one of the clan degrading herself by going out to service. Teaching a private school was the proper thing for an indigent gentlewoman. Sewing even, if done in the seclusion of home and not mentioned in public, could be tolerated. Story-writing was a genteel accomplishment and reflected credit upon the name. But leaving the paternal roof to wash other people's teacups, nurse other people's ails, and obey other people's orders for hire—this, this was degradation; and headstrong Louisa would disgrace her name forever if she did it.

Opposition only fired the revolutionary blood in my veins, and I crowned my iniquity by the rebellious declaration:

"If doing this work hurts my respectability, I wouldn't give much for it. My aristocratic ancestors don't feed or clothe me and my democratic ideas of honesty and honor won't let me be idle or dependent. You need not know me if you are ashamed of me, and I won't ask you for a penny; so, if I never do succeed in anything, I shall have the immense satisfaction of knowing I am under no obligation to any one."

In spite of the laughter and the lamentation, I got ready my small wardrobe, consisting of two calico dresses and one delaine, made by myself, also several large and uncompromising blue aprons and three tidy little sweeping-caps; for I had some English notions about housework and felt that my muslin hair-protectors would be useful in some of the "light labors" I was to undertake. It is needless to say they were very becoming. Then, firmly embracing my family, I set forth, one cold January day, with my little trunk, a stout heart, and a five-dollar bill for my fortune.

"She will be back in a week" was my sister's prophecy, as she wiped her weeping eye.

"No, she won't, for she has promised to stay the month out and she will keep her word," answered my mother, who always defended the black sheep of her flock.

I heard both speeches, and registered a tremendous vow to keep that promise, if I died in the attempt—little dreaming, poor innocent, what lay before me.

Josephus meantime had written me several remarkable letters, describing the different members of the family I was about to enter. His account was peculiar, but I believed every word of it and my romantic fancy was much excited by the details he gave. The principal ones are as follows, condensed from the voluminous epistles which he evidently enjoyed writing:

"You will find a stately mansion, fast falling to decay, for my father will have nothing repaired, preferring that the old house and its master should crumble away together. I have, however, been permitted to rescue a few rooms from ruin; and here I pass my recluse life, surrounded by the things I love. This will naturally be more attractive to you than the gloomy apartments my father inhabits, and I hope you will here allow me to minister to your young and cheerful nature when your daily cares are over. I need such companionship and shall always welcome you to my abode.

"Eliza, my sister, is a child at forty, for she has lived alone with my father and an old servant all her life. She is a good creature, but not lively, and needs stirring up, as you will soon see. Also I hope by your means to rescue her from the evil influence of Puah, who, in my estimation, is a *wretch*. She has gained entire control over Eliza, and warps her mind with great skill, prejudicing her against *me* and thereby desolating my home. Puah hates *me* and always has. Why I know not, except that I will not yield to her control. She ruled here for years while I was away, and my return upset all her nefarious plans. It will always be my firm opinion that she has tried to *poison me*, and may again. But even this dark suspicion will not deter me from my duty. I cannot send her away, for both my deluded father and my sister have entire faith in her, and I cannot shake it. She is faithful and kind to them, so I submit and remain to guard them, even at the risk of my life.

"I tell you these things because I wish you to know all and be warned, for this old hag has a specious tongue, 41 and I should grieve to see you deceived by her lies. Say nothing, but watch her silently, and help me to thwart her evil plots; but do not trust her, or beware."

Now this was altogether romantic and sensational, and I felt as if about to enter one of those delightfully dangerous houses we read of in novels, where perils, mysteries, and sins freely disport themselves, till the newcomer sets all to rights, after unheard of trials and escapes.

I arrived at twilight, just the proper time for the heroine to appear; and, as no one answered my modest solo on the rusty knocker, I walked in and looked about me. Yes, here was the long, shadowy hall, where the ghosts doubtless walked at midnight. Peering in at an open door on the right, I saw a parlor full of ancient furniture, faded, dusty, and dilapidated. Old portraits stared at me from the walls and a damp chill froze the marrow of my bones in the most approved style.

"The romance opens well," I thought, and, peeping in at an opposite door, beheld a luxurious apartment, full of the warm glow of firelight, the balmy breath of hyacinths and roses, the white glimmer of piano keys, and tempting rows of books along the walls.

The contrast between the two rooms was striking, and, after an admiring survey, I continued my explorations, thinking that I should not mind being "ministered to" in that inviting place when my work was done.

A third door showed me a plain, dull sitting room, with

an old man napping in his easy-chair. I heard voices in the kitchen beyond, and entering there, beheld Puah the fiend. Unfortunately, for the dramatic effect of the tableaux, all I saw was a mild-faced old woman, buttering toast, while she conversed with her familiar, a comfortable gray cat.

The old lady greeted me kindly, but I fancied her faded blue eye had a weird expression and her amiable words were all a snare, though I own I was rather disappointed at the commonplace appearance of this humble Borgia.

She showed me to a tiny room, where I felt more like a young giantess than ever, and was obliged to stow away my possessions as snugly as in a ship's cabin. When I presently descended, armed with a blue apron and "a heart for any fate," I found the old man awake and received from him a welcome full of ancient courtesy and kindliness. Miss Eliza crept in like a timid mouse, looking so afraid of her buxom companion that I forgot my own shyness in trying to relieve hers. She was so enveloped in shawls that all I could discover was that my mistress was a very nervous little woman, with a small button of pale hair on the outside of her head and the vaguest notions of work inside. A few spasmodic remarks and many awkward pauses brought me to teatime, when Josephus appeared, as tall, thin, and cadaverous as ever. After his arrival there was no more silence, for he preached all suppertime something in this agreeable style.

"My young friend, our habits, as you see, are of the simplest. We eat in the kitchen, and all together, in the primitive fashion; for it suits my father and saves labor. I could wish more order and elegance; but *my* wishes are not consulted and I submit I live above these petty crosses, and, though my health suffers from bad cookery, I do not murmur. Only, I must say, in passing, that if you *will* make your battercakes green with saleratus, Puah, I shall feel it my duty to throw them out of the window. *I* am used to poison; but I cannot see the coals of this blooming girl's stomach destroyed, as mine have been. And, speaking of duties, I may as well mention to you, Louisa (I call you so in a truly fraternal spirit), that I like to find my study in order when I come down in the morning; for I often need a few moments of solitude before I face the daily annoyances of my life. I shall permit *you* to perform this light task, for *you* have some idea of order (I see it in the formation of your brow), and feel sure that *you* will respect the sanctuary of thought. Eliza is so blind she does not see dust, and Puah enjoys devastating the one poor refuge I can call my own this side the grave. We are all waiting for you, sir. My father keeps up the old formalities, you observe; and I endure them, though *my* views are more advanced."

The old gentleman hastily finished his tea and returned thanks, when his son stalked gloomily away, evidently oppressed with the burden of his wrongs, also, as I irreverently fancied, with the seven "green" flapjacks he had devoured during the sermon.

I helped wash up the cups, and during that domestic rite Puah chatted in what I should have considered a cheery, social way had I not been darkly warned against her wiles.

"You needn't mind half Josephus says, my dear. He likes to hear himself talk and always goes on so before folks. I sometimes thinks his books and new ideas have sort of muddled his wits, for he is as full of notions as a paper is of pins; and he gets dreadfully put out if we don't give in to 'em. But, gracious me! they are so redicklus sometimes and so selfish I can't allow him to make a fool of himself or plague Lizy. She don't dare to say her soul is her own; so I have to stand up for her. His pa don't know half his odd doings; for I try to keep the old gentleman comfortable and have to manage 'em all, which is not an easy job I do assure you."

I had a secret conviction that she was right, but did not commit myself in any way, and we joined the social circle in the sitting room. The prospect was not a lively one, for the old gentleman nodded behind his newspaper. Eliza, with her head pinned up in a little blanket, slumbered on the sofa, Puah fell to knitting silently; and the plump cat dozed under the stove. Josephus was visible, artistically posed in the luxurious recesses of his cell, with the light 45 beaming on his thoughtful brow, as he pored over a large volume or mused with upturned eye.

Having nothing else to do, I sat and stared at him, till, emerging from a deep reverie, with an effective start, he became conscious of my existence and beckoned me to approach the "sanctuary of thought" with a dramatic waft of his large hand.

I went, took possession of an easy chair, and prepared myself for elegant conversation. I was disappointed, however; for Josephus showed me a list of his favorite dishes, sole fruit of all that absorbing thought, and, with an earnestness that flushed his saffron countenance, gave me hints as to the proper preparation of these delicacies.

I mildly mentioned that I was not a cook; but was effectually silenced by being reminded that I came to be generally useful, to take his sister's place, and see that the flame of life which burned so feebly in this earthly tabernacle was fed with proper fuel. Mince pies, Welsh rarebits, sausages, and strong coffee did not strike me as strictly spiritual fare; but I listened meekly and privately resolved to shift this awful responsibility to Puah's shoulders.

Detecting me in gape, after an hour of this high converse, he presented me with an overblown rose, which fell to pieces before I got out of the room, pressed my hand, and dismissed me with a fervent "God bless you, child. 46 Don't forget the dropped eggs for breakfast."

I was up betimes next morning and had the study in perfect order before the recluse appeared, enjoying a good prowl among the books as I worked and becoming so absorbed that I forgot the eggs, till a gusty sigh startled me, and I beheld Josephus, in dressing gown and slippers, languidly surveying the scene.

"Nay, do not fly," he said, as I grasped my duster in guilty haste. "It pleases me to see you here and lends a sweet, domestic charm to my solitary room. I like that graceful cap, that housewifely apron, and I beg you to wear them often; for it refreshes my eye to see something tasteful, young, and womanly about me. Eliza makes a bundle of herself and Puah is simply detestable."

He sank languidly into a chair and closed his eyes, as if the mere thought of his enemy was too much for him. I took advantage of this momentary prostration to slip away, convulsed with laughter at the looks and words of this bald-headed sentimentalist.

After breakfast I fell to work with a will, eager to show my powers and glad to put things to rights, for many hard jobs had evidently been waiting for a stronger arm than Puah's and a more methodical head than Eliza's.

Everything was dusty, moldy, shiftless, and neglected, except the domain of Josephus. Up-stairs the paper was dropping from the walls, the ancient furniture was all more or less dilapidated, and every hold and corner was full of relics tucked away by Puah, who was a regular old magpie. Rats and mice reveled in the empty rooms and spiders wove their tapestry undisturbed, for the old man would have nothing altered or repaired and his part of the house was fast going to ruin.

I longed to have a grand "clearing up"; but was forbidden to do more than to keep things in livable order. On the whole, it was fortunate, for I soon found that my hands would be kept busy with the realms of Josephus, whose ethereal being shrank from dust, shivered at a cold breath, and needed much cosseting with dainty food, hot fires, soft beds, and endless service, else, as he expressed it, the frail reed would break.

I regret to say that a time soon came when I felt supremely indifferent as to the breakage, and very skeptical as to the fragility of a reed that ate, slept, dawdled, and scolded so energetically. The rose that fell to pieces so suddenly was a good symbol of the rapid disappearance of all the romantic delusions I had indulged in for a time. A week's acquaintance with the inmates of this old house quite settled my opinion, and further developments only confirmed it.

Miss Eliza was a nonentity and made no more impression on me than a fly. The old gentleman passed his days in a placid sort of doze and took no notice of what went on about him. Puah had been a faithful drudge for years, and, instead of being a "wretch," was, as I soon satisfied myself, a motherly old soul, with no malice in her. The secret of Josephus's dislike was that the reverend tyrant ruled the house, and all obeyed him but Puah, who had nursed him as a baby, boxed his ears as a boy, and was not afraid of him even when he became a man and a minister. I soon repented of my first suspicions, and grew fond of her, for without my old gossip I should have fared ill when my day of tribulation came.

At first I innocently accepted the fraternal invitations to visit the study, feeling that when my days' work was done I earned a right to rest and read. But I soon found that this was not the idea. I was not to read; but to be read to. I was not to enjoy the flowers, pictures, fire, and books; but to keep them in order for my lord to enjoy. I was also to be a passive bucket, into which he was to pour all manner of philosophic, metaphysical, and sentimental rubbish. I was to serve his needs, soothe his sufferings, and sympathize with all his sorrows—be a galley slave, in fact.

As soon as I clearly understood this, I tried to put an end to it by shunning the study and never lingering there an instant after my work was done. But it availed little, for Josephus demanded much sympathy and was bound to have it. So he came and read poems while I washed dishes, discussed his pet problems all meal-times, and put reproachful notes under my door, in which were comically mingled complaints of neglect and orders for dinner.

I bore it as long as I could, and then freed my mind in

a declaration of independence, delivered in the kitchen, where he found me scrubbing the hearth. It was not an impressive attitude for an orator, nor was the occupation one a girl would choose when receiving calls; but I have always felt grateful for the intense discomfort of that moment, since it gave me the courage to rebel outright. Stranded on a small island of mat, in a sea of soapsuds, I brandished a scrubbing brush, as I indignantly informed him that I came to be a companion to his sister, not to him, and I should keep that post or none. This I followed up by reproaching him with the delusive reports he had given me of the place and its duties, and assuring him that I should not stay long unless matters mended.

"But I offer you lighter tasks, and you refuse them," he began, still hovering in the doorway, whither he had hastily retired when I opened my batteries.

"But I don't like the tasks, and consider them much worse than hard work" was my ungrateful answer, as I sat upon my island, with the softsoap conveniently near.

"Do you mean to say you prefer to scrub the hearth to sitting in my charming room while I read Hegel to you?" he demanded, glaring down upon me.

"Infinitely," I responded promptly, and emphasized my words by beginning to scrub with a zeal that made the bricks white with foam.

"Is it possible!" and, with a groan at my depravity, Josephus retired, full of ungodly wrath.

I remember that I immediately burst into jocund song, so that no doubt might remain in his mind, and continued to warble cheerfully till my task was done. I also remember that I cried heartily when I got to my room, I was so vexed, disappointed, and tired. But my bower was so small I should soon have swamped the furniture if I had indulged copiously in tears; therefore I speedily dried them up, wrote a comic letter home, and waited with interest to see what would happen next.

Far be it from me to accuse one of the nobler sex of spite or the small revenge of underhand annoyances and slights to one who could not escape and would not retaliate; but after that day a curious change came over the spirit of that very unpleasant dream. Gradually all the work of the house had been slipping into my hands; for Eliza was too poorly to help and direct, and Puah too old to do much besides the cooking. About this time I found that even the roughest work was added to my share, for Josephus was unusually feeble and no one was hired to do his chores. Having made up my mind to go when the month was out, I said nothing, but dug paths, brought water from the well, split kindlings, made fires, and sifted ashes, like a true Cinderella.

There never had been any pretense of companionship with Eliza, who spent her days muffling over the fire, and seldom exerted herself except to find odd jobs for me to do—rusty knives to clean, sheets to turn, old stockings to mend, and, when all else failed, some paradise of moths and mice to be cleared up; for the house was full of such "glory holds."

If I remonstrated, Eliza at once dissolved into tears and said she must do as she was told; Puah begged me to hold on till spring, when things would be much better; and pity pleaded for the poor souls. But I don't think I could have stood it if my promise had not bound me, for when the fiend said "Budge" honor said "Budge not" and I stayed.

But, being a mortal worm, I turned now and then when ireful Josephus trod upon me too hard, especially in the matter of boot-blacking. I really don't know why that is considered such humiliating work for a woman; but so it is, and there I drew the line. I would have cleaned the old man's shoes without a murmur; but he preferred to keep their native rustiness intact. Eliza never went out, and Puah affected carpet-slippers of the Chinese-junk pattern. Josephus, however, plumed himself upon his feet, which, like his nose, were large, and never took his walks abroad without having his boots in a high state of polish. He had brushed them himself at first; but soon after the explosion I discovered a pair of muddy boots in the shed, set suggestively near the blacking-box. I did not take the hint; feeling instinctively that this amiable being was trying how much I would bear for the sake of peace.

The boots remained untouched; and another pair soon

came to keep them company, whereat I smiled wickedly as I chopped just kindlings enough for my own use. Day after day the collection grew, and neither party gave in. Boots were succeeded by shoes, then rubbers gave a pleasing variety to the long line, and then I knew the end was near.

"Why are not my boots attended to?" demanded Josephus, one evening, when obliged to go out.

"I'm sure I don't know," was Eliza's helpless answer.

"I told Louizy I guessed you'd want some of 'em before long," observed Puah with an exasperating twinkle in her old eye.

"And what did she say?" asked my lord with an ireful whack of his velvet slippers as he cast them down.

"Oh! she said she was so busy doing your other work you'd have to do that yourself; and I thought she was about right."

"Louizy" heard it all through the slid, and could have embraced the old woman for her words, but kept still till Josephus had resumed his slippers with a growl and retired to the shed, leaving Eliza in tears, Puah chuckling, and the rebellious handmaid exulting in the china-closet.

Alas! for romance and the Christian virtues, several pairs of boots were cleaned that night, and my sinful soul enjoyed the spectacle of the reverend bootblack at his task. I even found my "fancy work," as I called the evening job of paring a bucketfull of hard russets with a dull 53 knife, much cheered by the shoe brush accompaniment played in the shed.

Thunder-clouds rested upon the martyr's brow at breakfast, and I was as much ignored as the cat. And what a relief that was! The piano was locked up, so were the bookcases, the newspapers mysteriously disappeared, and a solemn silence reigned at table, for no one dared to talk when that gifted tongue was mute. Eliza fled from the gathering storm and had a comfortable fit of neuralgia in her own room, where Puah nursed her, leaving me to skirmish with the enemy.

It was not a fair fight, and that experience lessened my respect for mankind immensely. I did my best however— grubbed about all day and amused my dreary evenings as well as I could; too proud even to borrow a book, lest it should seem like surrender. What a long month it was, and how eagerly I counted the hours of that last week, for my time was up Saturday and I hoped to be off at once. But when I announced my intention such dismay fell upon Eliza that my heart was touched, and Puah so urgently begged me to stay till they could get some one that I consented to remain a few days longer, and wrote posthaste to my mother, telling her to send a substitute quickly or I should do something desperate.

That blessed woman, little dreaming of all the woes I had endured, advised me to be patient, to do the generous thing, and be sure I should not regret it in the end. I groaned, submitted, and did regret it all the days of my life.

Three mortal weeks I waited; for, though two other victims came, I was implored to set them going, and tried to do it. But both fled after a day or two, condemning the place as a very hard one and calling me a fool to stand it another hour. I entirely agreed with them on both points, and, when I had cleared up after the second incapable lady, I tarried not for the coming of a third, but clutched my property and announced my departure by the next train.

Of course, Eliza wept, Puah moaned, the old man politely regretted, and the younger one washed his hands of the whole affair by shutting himself up in his room and forbidding me to say farewell because "he could not bear it." I laughed, and fancied it done for effect then; but I soon understood it better and did not laugh.

At the last moment, Eliza nervously tucked a sixpenny pocketbook into my hand and shrouded herself in the little blanket with a sob. But Puah kissed me kindly and whispered, with an odd look: "Don't blame us for anything. Some folks is liberal and some ain't." I thanked the poor old soul for her kindness to me and trudged gayly away to the station, whither my property had preceded me on a wheelbarrow, hired at my own expense.

I never shall forget that day. A bleak March afternoon, a sloppy, lonely road, and one hoarse crow stalking about 55 a field, so like Josephus that I could not resist throwing a snowball at him. Behind me stood the dull old house, no longer either mysterious or romantic in my disenchanted eyes; before me rumbled the barrow, bearing my dilapidated wardrobe; and in my pocket reposed what I fondly hoped was, if not a liberal, at least an honest return for seven weeks of the hardest work I ever did.

Unable to resist the desire to see what my earnings were, I opened the purse and beheld *four dollars*.

I have had a good many bitter minutes in my life; but one of the bitterest came to me as I stood there in the windy road, with the sixpenny pocket-book open before me, and looked from my poor chapped, grimy, chill-blained hands to the paltry sum that was considered reward enough for all the hard and humble labor they had done.

A girl's heart is a sensitive thing. And mine had been very full lately; for it had suffered many of the trials that wound deeply yet cannot be told; so I think it was but natural that my first impulse was to go straight back to that sacred study and fling this insulting money at the feet of him who sent it. But I was so boiling over with indignation that I could not trust myself in his presence, lest I should be unable to resist the temptation to shake him, in spite of his cloth.

No. I would go home, show my honorable wounds, tell 56 my pathetic tale, and leave my parents to avenge my wrongs. I did so; but over that harrowing scene I drop a veil, for my feeble pen refuses to depict the emotions of my outraged family. I will merely mention that the four dollars went back and the reverend Josephus never heard the last of it in that neighborhood.

My experiment seemed a dire failure and I mourned it as such for years; but more than once in my life I have been grateful for that serio-comico experience, since it has taught me many lessons. One of the most useful of these has been the power of successfully making a companion, not a servant, of those whose aid I need, and helping to gild their honest wages with the sympathy and justice which can sweeten the humblest and lighten the hardest task.

Transcendental
Wild Oats

On the first day of June, 184–, a large wagon, drawn by a small horse and containing a motley load, went lumbering over certain New England hills, with the pleasing accompaniments of wind, rain, and hail. A serene man with a serene child upon his knee was driving, or rather being driven, for the small horse had it all his own way. A brown boy with a William Penn style of countenance sat beside him, firmly embracing a bust of Socrates. Behind them was an energetic-looking woman, with a benevolent brow, satirical mouth, and eyes brimful of hope and courage. A baby reposed upon her lap, a mirror leaned against her knee, and a basket of provisions danced about at her feet, as she struggled with a large, unruly umbrella. Two blue-eyed little girls, with hands full of childish treasures, sat under one old shawl, chatting happily together.

In front of this lively party stalked a tall, sharp-featured man, in a long blue cloak; and a fourth small girl trudged along beside him through the mud as if she rather enjoyed it.

The wind whistled over the bleak hills; the rain fell in a despondent drizzle, and twilight began to fall. But the calm man gazed as tranquilly into the fog as if he beheld a radiant bow of promise spanning the gray sky. The cheery woman tried to cover every one but herself with the big umbrella. The brown boy pillowed his head on the bald pate of Socrates and slumbered peacefully. The little girls sang lullabies to their dolls in soft, maternal murmurs. The sharp-nosed pedestrian marched steadily on, with the blue cloak streaming out behind him like a banner; the lively infant splashed through the puddles with a duck-like satisfaction pleasant to behold.

Thus these modern pilgrims journeyed hopefully out of the old world, to found a new one in the wilderness.

The editors of *The Transcendental Tripod* had received from Messrs. Lion & Lamb (two of the aforesaid pilgrims) a communication from which the following statement is an extract:

"We have made arrangements with the proprietor of an estate of about a hundred acres which liberates this tract from human ownership. Here we shall prosecute our effort to initiate a Family in harmony with the primitive instincts of man.

"Ordinary secular farming is not our object. Fruit, grain, pulse, herbs, flax, and other vegetable products, receiving assiduous attention, will afford ample manual occupation, and chaste supplies for the bodily needs. It is intended to adorn the pastures with orchards, and to supersede the labor of cattle by the spade and the pruning-knife.

"Consecrated to human freedom, the land awaits the sober culture of devoted men. Beginning with small pecuniary means, this enterprise must be rooted in a reliance on the succors of an ever-bounteous Providence, whose vital affinities being secured by this union with uncorrupted field and unworldly persons, the cares and injuries of a life of gain are avoided.

"The inner nature of each member of the Family is at no time neglected. Our plan contemplates all such disciplines, cultures, and habits as evidently conduce to the purifying of the inmates.

"Pledged to the spirit alone, the founders anticipate no hasty or numerous addition to their numbers. The kingdom of peace is entered only through the gates of self-denial; and felicity is the test and the reward of loyalty to the unswerving law of Love."

This prospective Eden at present consisted of an old red farm-house, a dilapidated barn, many acres of meadow-land, and a grove. Ten ancient apple trees were all the "chaste supply" which the place offered as yet; but, in the firm belief that plenteous orchards were soon to be evoked from their inner consciousness, these sanguine founders had christened their domain Fruitlands.

Here Timon Lion intended to found a colony of Latter Day Saints, who, under his patriarchal sway, should regenerate the world and glorify his name for ever. Here Abel Lamb, with the devoutest faith in the high ideal which was to him a living truth, desired to plant a Paradise, where Beauty, Virtue, Justice, and Love might live happily together, without the possibility of a serpent entering in. And here his wife, unconverted but faithful to the end, hoped, after many wanderings over the face of the earth, to find rest for herself and a home for her children.

"There is our new abode," announced the enthusiast, smiling with a satisfaction quite undamped by the drops dripping from his hatbrim, as they turned at length into a cart-path that wound along a steep hillside into a barren-looking valley.

"A little difficult of access," observed his practical wife, as she endeavored to keep her various household gods from going overboard with every lurch of the laden ark.

"Like all good things. But those who earnestly desire and patiently seek will soon find us," placidly responded the philosopher from the mud, through which he was now endeavoring to pilot the much-enduring horse.

"Truth lies at the bottom of a well, Sister Hope," said Brother Timon, pausing to detach his small comrade from a gate, whereon she was perched for a clearer gaze into futurity.

"That's the reason we so seldom get at it, I suppose,"

replied Mrs. Hope, making a vain clutch at the mirror, which a sudden jolt sent flying out of her hands.

"We want no false reflections here," said Timon, with a grim smile, as he crunched the fragments under foot in his onward march.

Sister Hope held her peace, and looked wistfully through the mist at her promised home. The old red house with a hospitable glimmer at its windows cheered her eyes; and considering the weather, was a fitter refuge than the sylvan bowers some of the more ardent souls might have preferred.

The newcomers were welcomed by one of the elect precious—a regenerate farmer, whose idea of reform consisted chiefly in wearing white cotton raiment and shoes of untanned leather. This costume, with a snowy beard, gave him a venerable, and at the same time a somewhat bridal appearance.

The goods and chattels of the Society not having arrived, the weary family reposed before the fire on blocks of wood, while Brother Moses White regaled them with roasted potatoes, brown bread and water, in two plates, a tin pan, and one mug—his table service being limited. But, having cast the forms and vanities of a depraved world behind them, the elders welcomed hardship with the enthusiasm of new pioneers, and the children heartily enjoyed this foretaste of what they believed was to be a sort of perpetual picnic.

During the progress of this frugal meal, two more brothers appeared. One a dark, melancholy man, clad in homespun, whose particular mission was to turn his name hind part before and use as few words as possible. The other was a bland, bearded Englishman, who expected to be saved by eating uncooked food and going without clothes. He had not yet adopted the primitive costume, however; but contented himself with meditatively chewing dry beans out of a basket.

"Every meal should be a sacrament, and the vessels used beautiful and symbolical," observed Brother Lamb, mildly, righting the tin pan slipping about on his knees. "I priced a silver service when in town, but it was too costly; so I got some graceful cups and vases of Britannia ware."

"Hardest things in the world to keep bright. Will whiting be allowed in the community?" inquired Sister Hope, with a housewife's interest in labor-saving institutions.

"Such trivial questions will be discussed at a more fitting time," answered Brother Timon, sharply, as he burnt his fingers with a very hot potato. "Neither sugar, molasses, milk, butter, cheese, nor flesh are to be used among us, for nothing is to be admitted which has caused wrong or death to man or beast."

"Our garments are to be linen till we learn to raise our own cotton or some substitute for woollen fabrics," added Brother Abel, blissfully basking in an imaginary future as 66 warm and brilliant as the generous fire before him.

"Haou abaout shoes?" asked Brother Moses, surveying his own with interest.

"We must yield that point till we can manufacture an innocent substitute for leather. Bark, wood, or some durable fabric will be invented in time. Meanwhile, those who desire to carry out our idea to the fullest extent can go barefooted," said Lion, who liked extreme measures.

"I never will nor let my girls," murmured rebellious Sister Hope, under her breath.

"Haou do you cattle'ate to treat the ten-acre lot? Ef things ain't 'tended to right smart, we shan't hev no crops," observed the practical patriarch in cotton.

"We shall spade it," replied Abel, in such perfect good faith that Moses said no more, though he indulged in a shake of the head as he glanced at hands that had held nothing heavier than a pen for years. He was a paternal old soul and regarded the younger men as promising boys on a new sort of lark.

"What shall we do for lamps, if we cannot use any animal substance? I do hope light of some sort is to be thrown upon the enterprise," said Mrs. Lamb, with anxiety, for in those days kerosene and camphene were not, and gas unknown in the wilderness.

"We shall go without till we have discovered some vegetable oil or wax to serve us," replied Brother Timon, in a decided tone, which caused Sister Hope to resolve that 67 her private lamp should always be trimmed, if not burning.

"Each member is to perform the work for which experience, strength, and taste best fit him," continued Dictator Lion. "Thus drudgery and disorder will be avoided and harmony prevail. We shall arise at dawn, begin the day by bathing, followed by music, and then a chaste repast of fruit and bread. Each one finds congenial occupation till the meridian meal; when some deep-searching conversation gives rest to the body and development to the mind. Healthful labor again engages us till the last meal, when we assemble in social communion, prolonged till sunset, when we retire to sweet repose, ready for the next day's activity."

"What part of the work do you incline to yourself?" asked Sister Hope, with a humorous glimmer in her keen eyes.

"I shall wait till it is made clear to me. Being in preference to doing is the great aim, and this comes to us rather by a resigned willingness than a willful activity, which is a check to all divine growth," responded Brother Timon.

"I thought so." And Mrs. Lamb sighed audibly, for during the year he had spent in her family Brother Timon had so faithfully carried out his idea of "being, not doing," that she had found his "divine growth" both an 68 expensive and unsatisfactory process.

Here her husband struck into the conversation, his face shining with the light and joy of the splendid dreams and high ideals hovering before him.

"In these steps of reform, we do not rely so much on scientific reasoning or physiological skill as on the spirit's dictates. The greater part of man's duty consists in leaving alone much that he now does. Shall I stimulate with tea, coffee, or wine? No. Shall I consume flesh? Not if I value health. Shall I subjugate cattle? Shall I claim property in any created thing? Shall I trade? Shall I adopt a form of religion? Shall I interest myself in politics? To how many of these questions—could we ask them deeply enough and could they be heard as having relation to our eternal welfare—would the response be 'Abstain'?"

A mild snore seemed to echo the last word of Abel's rhapsody, for brother Moses had succumbed to mundane slumber and sat nodding like a massive ghost. Forest Absalom, the silent man, and John Pease, the English member, now departed to the barn; and Mrs. Lamb led her flock to a temporary fold, leaving the founders of the "Consociate Family" to build castles in the air till the fire went out and the symposium ended in smoke.

The furniture arrived next day, and was soon bestowed; for the principal property of the community consisted in books. To this rare library was devoted the best room in the house, and the few busts and pictures that still survived many flittings were added to beautify the sanctuary, for here the family was to meet for amusement, instruction, and worship.

Any housewife can imagine the emotions of Sister Hope, when she took possession of a large, dilapidated kitchen, containing an old stove and the peculiar stores out of which food was to be evolved for her little family of eleven. Cakes of maple sugar, dried peas and beans, barley and hominy, meal of all sorts, potatoes, and dried fruit. No milk, butter, cheese, tea, or meat, appeared. Even salt was considered a useless luxury and spice entirely forbidden by these lovers of Spartan simplicity. A ten years' experience of vegetarian vagaries had been good for training for this new freak, and her sense of the ludicrous supported her through many trying scenes.

Unleavened bread, porridge, and water for breakfast; bread, vegetables, and water for dinner, bread, fruit, and water for supper was the bill of fare ordained by the elders. No teapot profaned that sacred stove, no gory steak cried aloud for vengeance from her chaste gridiron; and only a brave woman's taste, time, and temper were sacrificed on that domestic altar.

The vexed question of light was settled by buying a quantity of bayberry wax for candles; and, on discovering that no one knew how to make them, pine knots were introduced, to be used when absolutely necessary. Being summer, the evenings were not long, and the weary fraternity found it no great hardship to retire with the birds.

The inner light was sufficient for most of them. But Mrs. Lamb rebelled. Evening was the only time she had to herself, and while the tired feet rested the skilful hands mended torn frocks and little stockings, or anxious heart forgot its burden in a book.

So "mother's lamp" burned steadily, while the philosophers built a new heaven and earth by moonlight; and through all the metaphysical mists and philanthropic pyrotechnics of that period Sister Hope played her own little game of "throwing light," and none but the moths were the worse for it.

Such farming probably was never seen before since Adam delved. The band of brothers began by spading garden and field; but a few days of it lessened their ardor amazingly. Blistered hands and aching backs suggested the expediency of permitting the use of cattle till the workers were better fitted for noble toil by a summer of the new life.

Brother Moses brought a yoke of oxen from his farm—at least, the philosophers thought so till it was discovered that one of the animals was a cow; and Moses confessed that he "must be let down easy, for he couldn't live on garden sarse entirely."

Great was Dictator Lion's indignation at this lapse from virtue. But time pressed, the work must be done; so the meek cow was permitted to wear the yoke and the recreant brother continued to enjoy forbidden draughts in 71 the barn, which dark proceeding caused the children to regard him as one set apart for destruction.

The sowing was equally peculiar, for, owing to some mistake, the three brethren, who devoted themselves to this graceful task, found when about half through the job that each had been sowing a different sort of grain in the same field; a mistake which caused much perplexity, as it could not be remedied; but, after a long consultation and a good deal of laughter, it was decided to say nothing and see what would come of it.

The garden was planted with a generous supply of useful roots and herbs; but, as manure was not allowed to profane the virgin soil, few of these vegetable treasures ever came up. Purslane reigned supreme, and the disappointed planters ate it philosophically, deciding that Nature knew what was best for them, and would generously supply their needs, if they could only learn to digest her "sallets" and wild roots.

The orchard was laid out, a little grafting done, new trees and vines set, regardless of the unfit season and entire ignorance of the husbandmen, who honestly believed that in the autumn they would reap a bounteous harvest.

Slowly things got into order, and rapidly rumors of the new experiment went abroad, causing many strange spirits to flock thither, for in those days communities were the fashion and transcendentalism raged wildly. Some came to

look on and laugh, some to be supported in poetic idleness, a few to believe sincerely and work heartily. Each member was allowed to mount his favorite hobby and ride it to his heart's content. Very queer were some of these riders, and very rampant some of the hobbies.

One youth, believing that language was of little consequence if the spirit was only right, startled newcomers by blandly greeting them with "good morning, damn you," and other remarks of an equally mixed order. A second irrepressible being held that all the emotions of the soul should be freely expressed, and illustrated his theory by antics that would have sent him to a lunatic asylum, if, as an unregenerate wag said, he had not already been in one. When his spirit soared, he climbed trees and shouted, when doubt assailed him, he lay down upon the floor and groaned lamentably. At joyful periods, he raced, leaped, and sang; when sad, he wept aloud; and when a great thought burst upon him in the watches of the night, he crowed like a jocund cockerel, to the great delight of the children and the great annoyance of the elders. One musical brother fiddled whenever so moved, sang sentimentally to the four little girls, and put a music-box on the wall when he hoed corn.

Brother Pease ground away at his uncooked food, or browsed over the farm on sorrel, mint, green fruit, and new vegetables. Occasionally he took his walks abroad, airily attired in an unbleached cotton *poncho*, which was the nearest approach to the primeval costume he was al- 73 lowed to indulge in. At midsummer he retired to the wilderness, to try his plan where the woodchucks were without prejudices and huckleberry bushes were hospitably full. A sunstroke unfortunately spoilt his plan, and he returned to semi-civilization a sadder and wiser man.

Forest Absalom preserved his Pythagorean silence, cultivated his fine dark locks, and worked like a beaver, setting an excellent example of brotherly love, justice, and fidelity by his upright life. He it was who helped overworked Sister Hope with her heavy washes, kneaded the endless succession of batches of bread, watched over the children, and did the many tasks left undone by the brethren, who were so busy discussing and defining great duties that they forgot to perform the small ones.

Moses White placidly plodded about, "chorin' raound," as he called it, looking like an old-time patriarch, with his silver hair and flowing beard, and saving the community from many a mishap by his thrift and Yankee shrewdness.

Brother Lion domineered over the whole concern; for, having put the most money into the speculation, he was resolved to make it pay—as if anything founded on an ideal basis could be expected to do so by any but enthusiasts.

Abel Lamb simply revelled in the Newness, firmly believing that this dream was to be beautifully realized, and in time not only little Fruitlands, but the whole earth, be turned into a Happy Valley. He worked with every muscle of his body, for *he* was in deadly earnest. He taught with his whole head and heart; planned and sacrificed, preached and prophesied, with a soul full of the purest aspirations, most unselfish purposes, and desires for a life devoted to God and man, too high and tender to bear the rough usage of this world.

It was a little remarkable that only one woman ever joined this community. Mrs. Lamb merely followed wheresoever her husband led—"as ballast for his balloon," as she said, in her bright way.

Miss Jane Gage was a stout lady of mature years, sentimental, amiable, and lazy. She wrote verses copiously, and had vague yearnings and graspings after the unknown, which led her to believe herself fitted for a higher sphere than any she had yet adorned.

Having been a teacher, she was set to instructing the children in the common branches. Each adult member took a turn at the infants; and, as each taught in his own way, the result was a chronic state of chaos in the minds of these much-afflicted innocents. Sleep, food, and poetic musings were the desires of dear Jane's life, and she shirked all duties as clogs upon her spirit's wings. Any thought of lending a hand with the domestic drudgery never occurred to her; and when to the question, "Are there any beasts of burden on the place?" Mrs. Lamb answered, with a face that told its own tale, "Only one woman!" the buxom Jane took no shame to herself, but laughed at the joke, and let the stout-hearted sister tug on alone.

Unfortunately, the poor lady hankered after the flesh-pots, and endeavored to stay herself with private sips of milk, crackers, and cheese, and on one dire occasion she partook of fish at a neighbor's table.

One of the children reported this sad lapse from the virtue, and poor Jane was publicly reprimanded by Timon.

"I only took a little bit of the tail," sobbed the penitent poetress.

"Yes, but the whole fish had to be tortured and slain that you might tempt your carnal appetite with that one taste of the tail. Know ye not, consumers of flesh meat, that ye are nourishing the wolf and tiger in your bosoms?"

At this awful question and the peal of laughter which arose from some of the younger brethren, tickled by the ludicrous contrast between the stout sinner, the stern judge, and the naughty satisfaction of the young detective, poor Jane fled from the room to pack her trunk, and return to a world were fishes' tails were not forbidden fruit.

Transcendental wild oats were sown broadcast that year, and the fame thereof has not yet ceased in the land; for, futile as this crop seemed to outsiders, it bore an invisible harvest, worth much to those who planted in earnest. As none of the members of this particular commu-

nity have ever recounted their experiences before, a few of

them may not be amiss, since the interest in these attempts has never died out and Fruitlands was the most ideal of all these castles in Spain.

A new dress was invented, since cotton, silk, and wool were forbidden as the product of slave-labor, worm-slaughter, and sheep-robbery. Tunics and trowsers of brown linen were the only wear. The women's skirts were longer, and their straw hat-brims wider than the men's and this was the only difference. Some persecution lent a charm to the costume, and the long-haired, linen-clad reformers quite enjoyed the mild martyrdom they endured when they left home.

Money was abjured, as the root of all evil. The produce of the land was to supply most of their wants, or be exchanged for the few things they could not grow. This idea had its conveniences; but self-denial was the fashion, and it was surprising how many things one can do without. When they desired to travel, they walked, if possible, begged the loan of a vehicle, or boldly entered car or coach, and, stating their principles to the officials, took the consequences. Usually their dress, their earnest frankness, and gentle resolution won them a passage; but now and then they met with hard usage, and had the satisfaction of suffering for their principles.

On one of these penniless pilgrimages they took passage on a boat, and, when fare was demanded, artlessly offered to talk, instead of pay. As the boat was well under way and they actually had not a cent, there was no help for it. So Brothers Lion and Lamb held forth to the assembled passengers in their most eloquent style. There must have been something effective in this conversation, for the listeners were moved to take up a contribution for these inspired lunatics, who preached peace on earth and goodwill to man so earnestly, with empty pockets. A goodly sum was collected; but when the captain presented it the reformers proved that they were consistent even in their madness, for not a penny would they accept, saying, with a look at the group about them, whose indifference or contempt had changed to interest and respect, "You see how well we get on without money," and so went serenely on their way, with their linen blouses flapping airily in the bold October wind.

They preached vegetarianism everywhere and resisted all temptations of the flesh, contentedly eating apples and bread at well-spread tables, and much afflicting hospitable hostesses by denouncing their food and taking away their appetites, discussing the "horrors of shambles," the "incorporation of the brute in man," and "on elegant abstinence the sign of a pure soul." But, when the perplexed or offended ladies asked what they should eat, they got in reply a bill of fare consisting of "bowls of sunrise for breakfast," "solar seeds of the sphere," "dishes from Plutarch's chaste table," and other viands equally hard to find in any modern market.

Reform conventions of all sorts were haunted by these brethren, who said many wise things and did many foolish ones. Unfortunately, these wanderings interfered with their harvest at home; but the rule was to do what the spirit moved, so they left their crops to Providence and went a-reaping in wider and, let us hope, more fruitful fields than their own.

Luckily, the earthly providence who watched over Abel Lamb was at hand to glean the scanty crop yielded by the "uncorrupted land," which, "consecrated to human freedom," had received "the sober culture of devout men."

About the same time the grain was ready to house, some call of the Oversoul wafted all the men away. An easterly storm was coming up and the yellow stacks were sure to be ruined. Then Sister Hope gathered her forces. Three little girls, one boy (Timon's son), and herself, harnessed to clothes-baskets and Russia-linen sheets, were the only teams she could command; but with these poor appliances the indomitable woman got in the grain and saved food for her young, with the instinct and energy of a mother-bird with a brood of hungry nestlings to feed.

This attempt at regeneration had its tragic as well as comic side, though the world only saw the former.

With the first frosts, the butterflies, who had sunned themselves in the new light through the summer, took flight, leaving the few bees to see what honey they had stored for winter use. Precious little appeared beyond the satisfaction of a few months of holy living.

At first it seemed as if a chance to try holy dying was also to be offered them. Timon, much disgusted with the failure of the scheme, decided to retire to the Shakers, who seemed to be the only successful community going.

"What is to become of us?" asked Mrs. Hope, for Abel was heart-broken at the bursting of his lovely bubble.

"You can stay here, if you like, till a tenant is found. No more wood must be cut, however, and no more corn ground. All I have must be sold to pay the debts of the concern, as the responsibility is mine" was the cheering reply.

"Who is to pay us for what we have lost? I gave all I had—furniture, time, strength, six months of my children's lives—and all are wasted. Abel gave himself body and soul, and is almost wrecked by hard work and disappointment. Are we to have no return for this, but leave to starve and freeze in an old house, with winter at hand, no money, and hardly a friend left, for this wild scheme has alienated nearly all we had. You talk much about justice. Let us have a little, since there is nothing else left."

But the woman's appeal met with no reply but the old one: "It was an experiment. We all risked something, and must bear our loses as we can."

With this cold comfort, Timon departed with his son, and was absorbed into the Shaker brotherhood, where he soon found that the order of things was reversed, and it was all work and no play.

Then the tragedy began for the forsaken little family. Desolation and despair fell upon Abel. As his wife said, his new beliefs had alienated many friends. Some thought him mad, some unprincipled. Even the most kindly thought him a visionary, whom it was useless to help till he took more practical views of life. All stood aloof, saying: "Let him work out his own ideas, and see what they are worth."

He had tried, but it was a failure. The world was not ready for Utopia yet, and those who attempted to found it only got laughed at for their pains. In other days, men could sell all and give to the poor, lead lives devoted to holiness and high thought, and after the persecution was over, find themselves honored as saints or martyrs. But in modern times these things are out of fashion. To live for one's principles, at all costs, is a dangerous speculation; and the failure of an ideal, no matter how humane and noble, is harder for the world to forgive and forget than bank robbery or the grand swindles of corrupt politicians.

Deep waters now for Abel, and for a time there seemed no passage through. Strength and spirits were exhausted by hard work and too much thought. Courage failed when, looking about for help, he saw no sympathizing face, no hand outstretched to help him, no voice to say cheerily: 81

"We all make mistakes, and it takes many experiences to shape a life. Try again, and let us help you."

Every door was closed, every eye averted, every heart cold, and no way open whereby he might earn bread for his children. His principles would not permit him to do many things that others did; and in the few fields where conscience would allow him to work, who would employ a man who had flown in the face of society, as he had done?

Then this dreamer, whose dream was the life of his life, resolved to carry out his idea to the bitter end. There seemed no place for him here—no work, no friend. To go begging conditions was as ignoble as to go begging money. Better perish of want than sell one's soul for the sustenance of his body. Silently he lay down upon his bed, turning his face to the wall, and waited with pathetic patience for death to cut the knot which he could not untie. Days and nights went by, and neither food nor water passed his lips. Soul and body were dumbly struggling together, and no word of complaint betrayed what either suffered.

His wife, when tears and prayers were unavailing, sat down to wait the end with a mysterious awe and submission; for in this entire resignation of all things there was an eloquent significance to her who knew him as no other human being did.

"Leave all to God" was his belief; and in this crisis the

loving soul clung to his faith, sure that the All-wise Father would not desert this child who tried to live so near to Him. Gathering her children about her, she waited the issue of the tragedy that was being enacted in that solitary room, while the first snow fell outside, untrodden by the footprints of a single friend.

But the strong angels who sustain and teach perplexed and troubled souls came and went, leaving no trace without, but working miracles within. For, when all other sentiments had faded into dimness, all other hopes died utterly; when the bitterness of death was nearly over, when the body was past any pang of hunger or thirst, and soul stood ready to depart, the love that outlives all else refused to die. Head had bowed to defeat, hand had grown weary with too heavy tasks, but heart could not grow cold to those who live in its tender depths, even when death touched it.

"My faithful wife, my little girls—they have not forsaken me, they are mine by ties that none can break. What right have I to leave them alone? What right to escape from the burden and the sorrow I have helped to bring? This duty remains to me, and I must do it manfully. For their sakes, the world will forgive me in time; for their sakes, God will sustain me now."

Too feeble to rise, Abel groped for the food that always lay within his reach, and in the darkness and solitude of that memorable night ate and drank what was to him the 83 bread and wine of a new communion, a new dedication of heart and life to the duties that were left him when the dreams fled.

In the early dawn, when that sad wife crept fearfully to see what change had come to the patient face on the pillow, she found it smiling at her, saw a wasted hand outstretched to her, and heard a feeble voice cry bravely, "Hope!"

What passed in that little room is not to be recorded except in the hearts of those who suffered and endured much for love's sake. Enough for us to know that soon the wan shadow of a man came forth, leaning on the arm that never failed him, to be welcomed and cherished by the children, who never forgot the experiences of that time.

"Hope" was the watchword now; and, while the last logs blazed on the hearth, the last bread and apples covered the table, the new commander, with recovered courages, said to her husband:

"Leave all to God—and me. He has done his part; now I will do mine."

"But we have no money, dear."

"Yes, we have. I sold all we could spare, and have enough to take us away from this snowbank."

"Where can we go?"

"I have engaged four rooms at our good neighbor,

Lovejoy's. There we can live cheaply till spring. Then for new plans and a home of our own, please God."

"But, Hope, your little store won't last long, and we have no friends."

"I can sew and you can chop wood. Lovejoy offers you the same pay as he gives his other men; my old friend, Mrs. Truman, will send me all the work I want; and my blessed brother stands by us to the end. Cheer up, dear heart, for while there is work and love in the world we shall not suffer."

"And while I have my good angel Hope, I shall not despair, even if I wait another thirty years before I step beyond the circle of the sacred little world in which I still have a place to fill."

So one bleak December day, with their few possessions piled on an ox-sled, the rosy children perched atop, and the parents trudging arm in arm behind, the exiles left their Eden and faced the world again.

"Ah, me! my happy dream. How much I leave behind that never can be mine again," said Abel, looking back at the lost Paradise, lying white and chill in its shroud of snow.

"Yes, dear; but how much we bring away," answered brave-hearted Hope, glancing from husband to children.

"Poor Fruitlands! the name was as great a failure as the rest!" continued Abel, with a sigh, as a frost-bitten apple fell from a leafless bough at his feet.

But the sigh changed to a smile as his wife added, in a half-tender, half-satirical tone:

"Don't you think Apple Slump would be a better name for it, dear?"

LOUISA MAY ALCOTT · *An Old-Fashioned Thanksgiving and Other Stories*

HANS CHRISTIAN ANDERSEN · *The Emperor's New Clothes*

J. M. BARRIE · *Peter Pan in Kensington Gardens*

WILLIAM BLAKE · *Songs of Innocence and Experience*

GEOFFREY CHAUCER · *The Wife of Bath and Other Canterbury Tales*

ANTON CHEKHOV · *The Black Monk* and *Peasants*

SAMUEL TAYLOR COLERIDGE · *The Rime of the Ancient Mariner*

COLETTE · *Gigi*

JOSEPH CONRAD · *Youth*

ROALD DAHL · *Lamb to the Slaughter and Other Stories*

ROBERTSON DAVIES · *A Gathering of Ghost Stories*

FYODOR DOSTOYEVSKY · *The Grand Inquisitor*

SIR ARTHUR CONAN DOYLE · *The Man with the Twisted Lip* and *The Adventure of the Devil's Foot*

RALPH WALDO EMERSON · *Nature*

OMER ENGLEBERT (TRANS.) · *The Lives of the Saints*

FANNIE FARMER · *The Original 1896 Boston Cooking-School Cook Book*

EDWARD FITZGERALD (TRANS.) · *The Rubáiyát of Omar Khayyám*

ROBERT FROST · *The Road Not Taken and Other Early Poems*

GABRIEL GARCÍA MÁRQUEZ · *Bon Voyage, Mr President and Other Stories*

NIKOLAI GOGOL · *The Overcoat* and *The Nose*

GRAHAM GREENE · *Under the Garden*

JACOB AND WILHELM GRIMM · *Grimm's Fairy Tales*

NATHANIEL HAWTHORNE · *Young Goodman Brown and Other Stories*

O. HENRY · *The Gift of the Magi and Other Stories*

WASHINGTON IRVING · *Rip Van Winkle* and *The Legend of Sleepy Hollow*

HENRY JAMES · *Daisy Miller*

V. S. VERNON JONES (TRANS.) · *Aesop's Fables*

JAMES JOYCE · *The Dead*

GARRISON KEILLOR · *Truckstop and Other Lake Wobegon Stories*

FOR THE BEST IN PAPERBACKS, LOOK FOR THE

In every corner of the world, on every subject under the sun, Penguin represents quality and variety—the very best in publishing today.

For complete information about books available from Penguin—including Puffins, Penguin Classics, and Arkana—and how to order them, write to us at the appropriate address below. Please note that for copyright reasons the selection of books varies from country to country.

In the United States: Please write to *Consumer Sales, Penguin USA, P.O. Box 999, Dept. 17109, Bergenfield, New Jersey 07621-0120.* VISA and MasterCard holders call 1-800-253-6476 to order all Penguin titles.

In Canada: Please write to *Penguin Books Canada Ltd, 10 Alcorn Avenue, Suite 300, Toronto, Ontario M4V 3B2.*

In the United Kingdom: Please write to *Dept. JC, Penguin Books Ltd, FREEPOST, West Drayton, Middlesex UB7 OBR.*